This book belongs to:

Waking Up Down Under

by
CAROL VOTAW
illustrated by
SUSAN BANTA

NORTHWORD
Minnetonka, Minnesota

The illustrations were created using acrylics on vellum surface Bristol
The text and display type were set in Big Caslon and Berkeley Oldstyle
Composed in the United States of America
Art directed and designed by Lois A. Rainwater
Edited by Kristen McCurry

Books for Young Readers

11571 K-Tel Drive
Minnetonka, MN 55343
www.tnkidsbooks.com

Library of Congress Cataloging-in-Publication Data

Votaw, Carol.
Waking up down under / By Carol Votaw ; Illustrated by Susan Banta.
p. cm.
ISBN 978-1-55971-976-6 (hc)
1. Animals--Australia--Juvenile literature. I. Banta, Susan. II. Title.

QL338.V68 2007

591.994--dc22 2006101500

Printed in Singapore
10 9 8 7 6 5 4 3 2 1

To Mom and Dad, for stretching my horizons
by sharing their love of reading

—C. J. V.

In memory of my Father

—S. F. B.

Look who's waking up
In a land far away,
Where your starry night
Is their sunny day.

Wake up, kookaburra,
The sun is sleeping late.
Sound your merry laughing call,
My rowdy cheerful mate!

Wake up, little joey,
You have the perfect seat
To spy a pair of extra-large,
Awesome leaping feet.

Wake up, fairy penguin,
Waddle from your nest.
A burrow may be warm and snug,
But diving is the best!

Wake up, smiling dolphin,
Frolic in the sun.
Come roll with the giant waves
And leap just for fun!

Wake up, rainbow lorikeet,
The sun is in the sky.
Spread your magic-colored wings.
Make a rainbow fly.

Wake up, little emu,
Nibble in the sun.
Your feathers may not fly,
But oh, how you can run!

What a busy day it's been,
Sunlight fades away.
Cuddle up my sleepy ones,
The moon is here to stay.

Now the stars are shining,
Is it time for bed?
A nocturnal fellow
Shakes his furry head.

Wake up, young koala,
Feel the twilight breeze.
Climb a tree; it's time to munch
On eucalyptus leaves.

Wake up, spiny fellow,
Catch a termite snack.
Echidna, you're so cute,
Though prickly on your back!

Wake up, little bilby,
The desert evening's come.
Hear the pitter-patter
Of insects on the run.

Wake up, bashful platypus,
From your daily nap.
Dive for worms and tasty shrimp,
You furry, duck-billed chap!

Wake up, cuddly wombat,
Great tunnel engineer.
Graze beneath a starry sky,
All is calm and clear.

Wake up, sugar glider,
Spread your body wide.
Let go of the tallest tree
And take a starlit ride.

What a crew of creatures,
What a bunch of fun!
Some wake with the rising moon
And some wake with the sun.

ALL THE ANIMALS IN THIS BOOK MAKE THEIR HOME IN AUSTRALIA.

Kookaburra

The kookaburra is famous for its loud, laughing call. It is the world's largest kingfisher. Kookaburras eat snakes, lizards, fish, and small birds. According to native Australian legend, the kookaburra laughs each morning to remind the sky spirits to light the great fire in the sky.

Rainbow Lorikeet

This striking bird has green, orange, blue, red, violet, and yellow feathers – all the colors in a rainbow! It is about twelve inches long and eats flowers, fruits, and berries.

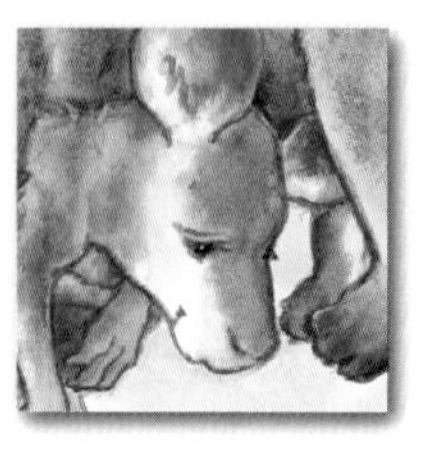

Kangaroo

Kangaroos are marsupials. This means they carry their young in a pouch. Kangaroo babies are called joeys. Red kangaroos are the largest marsupial.

Emu

Emus are large, ostrich-like birds. They can't fly, but they run very fast. Emus have droopy feathers that bounce as they run. They eat grass, flowers, and sometimes insects.

Fairy Penguin

The fairy penguin is the smallest penguin. Instead of living on snow and ice, fairy penguins live in burrows on land. They spend their days at sea diving for small fish, squid, and krill, which look like shrimp.

Koala

This marsupial lives in the forest. Koalas don't need to drink water because they get enough water from the eucalyptus leaves they eat. Their name comes from a native Australian saying that means "no drink."

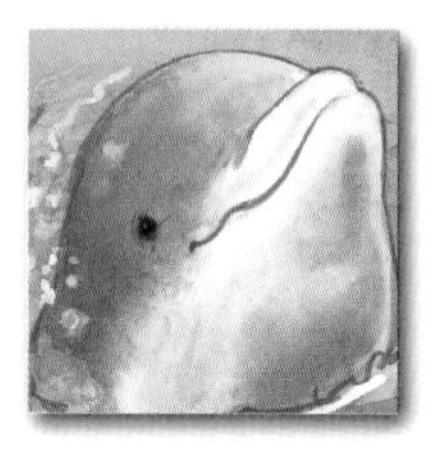

Dolphin

Bottlenose dolphins are very sociable. They swim in groups called pods. Dolphins enjoy chasing each other, touching each other, and making sounds. They swim by moving their flukes up and down. Flukes are tail fins!

Echidna

This prickly animal, pronounced i-kid-na, has a long, sticky tongue to catch termites and ants. Echidnas are mammals that lay one leathery egg a year. The female nurses her baby in a pouch until the little echidna grows too prickly. Ouch! Then she digs a burrow where she feeds her little one for six months.

Bilby

A bilby is a marsupial about the size of a rabbit. Bilbies eat little bugs. Their big ears help them locate insects by sound at night. Bilbies used to be common in Australia, but now they are endangered. Australian children get chocolate bilbies for Easter.

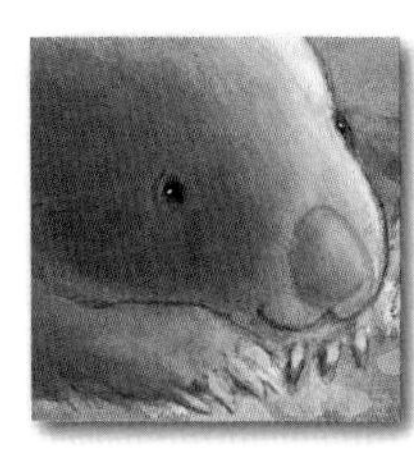

Wombat

Wombats look like little bears and weigh almost 90 pounds. They are expert burrowers and come out in the cool evenings to graze. Wombats are marsupials, too, but their pouch opens at the back instead of the front, so dirt doesn't fill their pouch as they dig!

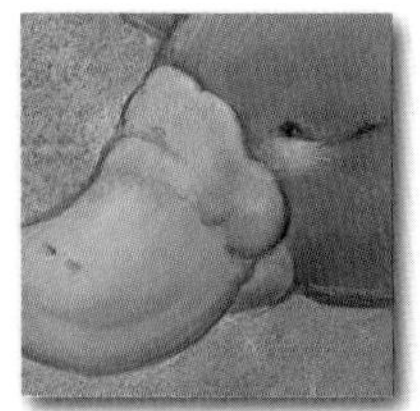

Platypus

What an unusual animal! The platypus is a mammal with a rubbery bill, webbed feet, and dense fur. Females lay soft, leathery eggs and have milk glands to feed their young. Males have a poisonous spur on their ankles, which they use to poke others that get in their way.

Sugar Glider

Sugar gliders have a thin skin that stretches between their front and hind legs. This skin acts like a wing and allows them to glide from tree to tree! Because they eat the sweet nectar of flowers, this little marsupial was named a sugar glider.

CAROL VOTAW earned a B.A. from St. Mary's College, where she studied history, art, and music, and an M.B.A. from Indiana University. She has worked in advertising and now writes children's stories and teaches piano. Carol lives in Rochester Hills, Michigan, with her husband and two daughters. In her spare time, she enjoys kayaking, sailing, skiing, and mountain biking with her family. *Waking Up Down Under* is her second children's book.

SUSAN BANTA was born in Washington, D.C., but grew up in Montreal. She earned a degree in fine arts from Syracuse University and explored various careers, including fashion illustration and book production. She has illustrated lots of educational material and thirty books. Susan and her husband, a retired librarian, now live in Brookfield, Vermont. When not at the drawing board she likes to read, quilt, garden, or strap on her snowshoes or cross-country skis.